Ming
and the
Magic Kite

by
Grammy Lo

Follow Your dreams!

illustrated by
Rebecca Pearl

ISBN: 978-1-939300-13-3

Library of Congress Card Catalog Number: 2013942225

Ming and the Magic Kite

author:	Grammy "Lo" Lois B. Noffsinger Spurrier
illustrator:	Rebecca Pearl
book design:	Glenda Tarazon Krouse

Printed by HPNbooks

president:	Ron Lammert
administration:	Donna M. Mata
	Melissa G. Quinn
book sales:	Dee Steidle
production:	Colin Hart

www.hpnbooks.com

Ming and the Magic Kite is the first in a series of illustrated children's books.
For more information, please contact the author at 240-674-6642.

To Rebecca Pearl,
A wonderful friend
and soul sister. Her
art is an inspiration!
She is blessed with a
great talent!

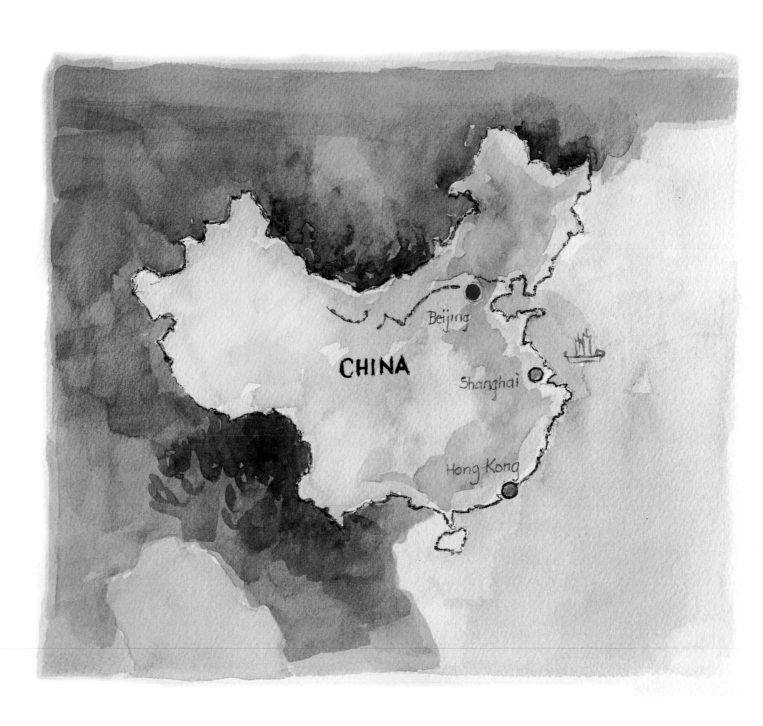

A long time ago

in a far off land called China,

there lived a little boy

named Ming.

Ming was born with

one leg shorter than the other.

Since Ming walks with a limp,

he was not allowed to go fishing

with the men of the village.

Ming had to stay home

and help the women.

He gathered wood.

He stirred the rice.

He made rice paper

and he loved to draw.

One day a soldier of the Emperor

came to the village on a beautiful black horse.

He blew a trumpet and announced

there would be a contest.

The person who created the most beautiful

kite and the one that flew the highest

would win a trip to the

Imperial Palace of the Emperor.

At the Emperor's palace,

all of the winners would compete

for a large fishing boat.

Ming made a kite

that looked like a golden fish.

He cut the fish out of rice paper

and glued all of the sides together

except for the mouth.

He put a strong piece of paper

inside the mouth.

He found very thin
pieces of abalone shell and
glued them to the fish kite.
The fish glimmered in the sun
and flew very high in the sky.
Ming and his family went
to the Emperor's palace,
where the competition
was to take place.

On the day of the contest,

the clouds filled the sky.

Kites from all over the kingdom filled the air.

Ming's kite was the last one to go up in the air.

The wind picked up and the sun came out.

Ming's kite flew the highest.

The brilliant sun made

Ming's kite glow in the sky.

Ming won the kite contest

and the magnificent fishing boat.

Ming became the captain of the ship.

He and his family

lived happily ever after.

When Ming returned home,

he wrote a beautiful song about his kite.

"The Magic Song"

Oh, magic kite please fly for me

Over the land and over the sea

Fly through the air so very high

You bring me joy as the days go by

The Magic Kite by Grammy 'Lo'

Oh Magic Kite Please Fly For Me

O ver The Land And O ver the Sea

Fly Through the Air So ver-y High

you Bring Me joy As the Days go By

'Key of C'

C · · · A · C · · A · · C · · A · G · F
Oh magic Kite Please Fly for Me

C · · A · · C · A · CA · G · F
Over The land and over the sea

A · · A · F · · A · F · · A F · C
Fly through the air so very high

C · A · · C · A · · A C · · A · G · F
You bring me joy as the days go by.

Song by Grammy 'Lo'

Music brings joy to the Soul!

25

This kite was drawn by

the artist of this book.

Use the three blank pages

to draw your own kite!

⌘

⌘

⌘

⌘

⌘

⌘

⌘

About the Author

Grammy "Lo" Lois B. Noffsinger Spurrier

Grammy "Lo" Lois B. Noffsinger Spurrier

was born in Frederick, Maryland in 1941.

She married Charles Noffsinger

a dairy farmer in 1962.

Lois graduated from Hood College

and taught kindergarten for forty-five years.

Grammy "Lo" still teaches music to three and

four year olds at Good Shepherd Preschool.

Lois has four sons, one daughter

and twelve grandchildren.

She still owns a farm in

Frederick County, Maryland.

About the Illustrator

Rebecca Pearl

Rebecca Pearl is a well known Maryland artist. At 61 she is an accomplished painter and teaches in her own gallery in Emmitsburg.

In 2006 after completing a commissioned work of a mounted policeman she was able to adopt a retired US Park Police horse named Gilbert.

"This event changed my life in body, mind and soul. Since that time I have become fit and healthy, ride about three times per week and take my horse to a dressage riding lesson once a week. Having the blessing of Gilbert in my life has taught me many things, and that is why I wrote and illustrated, *Gilbert and the Great Horse Spirit*. Enjoy!"

Rebecca resides near the Catoctin Mountains with her husband, 2 German Shepherds, 3 cats and of course, 2 horses.